DAD,
DOES GOD EXIST?

CHARLIE H. CAMPBELL

Illustrated by Julia Veenstra

GOD BLESS
YOU SCRIPTURE
FAMILY!
[signature]
3 JOHN v. 2

For Selah, Addison, Caden, Emerie, Ryland and every other child growing up in a world that will challenge their belief in God and the Bible. Also, a very special thank you to my good friend Rob Nash—without whom this book would not be.
—Charlie

I dedicate this book to the Lord Jesus—my Rock, my husband Doug, who continues to amaze me with his depth, my five wonderful children who inspire me, Rachel, Joel, Aaron, Noah, and Abigail, and Arnold and Dini Veenstra, my firm foundation.
—Julia

DAD, DOES GOD EXIST?

Text Copyright © 2007, 2017 by Charlie H. Campbell
Illustrations © 2007, 2017 by Julia Veenstra

Published in 2017 by The Always Be Ready Apologetics Ministry
P. O. Box 130342, Carlsbad, CA 92013
Email: info@alwaysbeready.com

Additional copies of this book can be found at **AlwaysBeReady.com.**

ISBN: 978-1495243127

Printed in the United States of America.

"FOR EVER SINCE

the world was created, people have seen the earth and sky. Through everything God made, they can clearly see His invisible qualities—His eternal power and divine nature. So they have no excuse for not knowing God." (Romans 1:20)

Hi, my name is Sarah. This is Thomas. He is one of my best friends at school.

The other day he told me something that shocked me. Thomas said, "God doesn't exist, Sarah. People just made Him up."

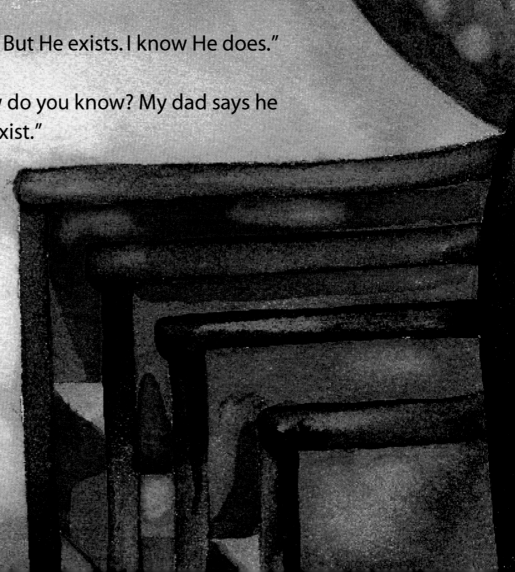

I asked Thomas, "Who told you that?" He replied, "My dad. He's a scientist."

"Well, He *does* exist," I told him.

Thomas said, "I can't see Him. Can you see Him?"

I answered him, "No. But He exists. I know He does."

Thomas asked, "How do you know? My dad says he knows God *doesn't* exist."

I informed him that my dad would know the answer and that I was going to ask him.

Later that night, as my dad was putting me to bed, I said, "Dad, my friend Thomas claims that God doesn't exist. His dad told him that people just made up God and that He's not real."

My dad responded, "There are people in the world Sarah who don't believe in God. They are called atheists." That was a big word, but I found out that "atheist" is a word to describe people who do not believe God exists.

"Dad? How do we know that God *does* exist?"

My dad answered, "That is a great question Sarah. I'll tell you what, why don't you get out of bed, put on your slippers for a couple minutes, and come with me out into the backyard."

"Yippee!—I love staying up late!" (Maybe I'll ask my dad these big questions more often!)

My dad said, "I want to show you something. Do you see those stars there in the sky?"

"Yes."

He asked me, "How do you think they got there?"

I told him, "God made them."

Dad told me that was right. Then he said, "The very first verse in the Bible tells us, 'In the beginning God created the heavens and the Earth (Genesis 1:1).' Now, let me ask you a question. Could those stars have gotten there without a creator?"

I told him, "I don't think so."

"The heavens tell of the glory of God. The skies display His marvelous craftsmanship."
(Psalm 19:1)

He said, "It would be impossible. Before the universe and the stars existed, they weren't around. The planets and the stars didn't exist. And something can't just come from nothing. Atheists believe that at one point, a long time ago, there was nothing and then all of a sudden the stars and planets sprang into existence all by themselves, with no God."

I laughed, "That's silly!".

My dad said, "Right. Can nothing make something Sarah?"

"No," I responded.

My dad asked, "Why not?"

"Nothing can't do anything!" I exclaimed. "It can't see, smell, act, or think. Nothing can't even create an ant! So, there's no way nothing could create enormous stars, planets, moons, and mountains!"

My dad laughed, "That's right Sarah. Everything we can see has a maker doesn't it? See that big ball over there? Did somebody make that ball or might it have come into existence all on its own?"

I said, "Someone made it!"

My dad agreed, "Right! Have you ever *seen* the person who made it?"

I answered, "No."

My dad explained, "The same is true with God. We can't see Him, but we look at the stars and the moon, and the planets, and we know that someone made them. They couldn't have just brought themselves into existence. Now, let's head back inside. It's cold!"

"Thanks Dad."

After we got inside, my dad told me, "Go grab our photo album from our family vacation last summer." My dad asked, "See that photo? What is that a picture of?"

That was easy. "Mount Rushmore. That was from our trip to South Dakota last year."

My dad said, "Yes. See those faces there in the rock?"

"Yes."

My dad asked, "How did those get there?"

"I don't know."

My dad asked me, "What if I was to tell you that over millions of years the wind and the rain carved those faces there in the rock? What would you think? Would you believe me?"

I laughed, "Nooo. That's not how they got there."

My dad said, "I know. We realize that somebody carved those faces there don't we?"

I said, "Yes."

My dad explained, "Atheists believe that something incredible took place. They believe over millions of years, the effects of nature created real, living, breathing people.
Not rock people (like Mount Rushmore), but real people with 206 bones, 640 muscles, and hearts that beat over 100,000 times a day."

I told him, "That sounds ridiculous!"

My dad said, "Right. God thinks that's ridiculous also. God says that it's foolish to not believe in Him (Psalm 14:1). God says the evidence for His existence is all around us."

My dad went on, "Sarah, the existence of the stars and planets, and incredibly complex living creatures isn't the only evidence God exists. Two thousand years ago, God came to the Earth for people to see Him."

I said, "That was Jesus."

My Dad continued, "That's right. We know Jesus was God, not just because He told us He was (John 5:18), but because He did amazing things that only God could do. What are some of the things Jesus did to prove He was God?"

I said, "Jesus performed miracles. He opened the eyes of people who were blind."

"Great. What else?" my dad asked.

I said, "He cured people who couldn't walk, and helped them to leap up and dance for joy."

My dad said, "Good! He also healed lepers. He raised people who had died back to life. He lived a sinless life."

I added, "He walked on water!"

My dad smiled, "You're my little Bible scholar! He even raised Himself back to life after He died on the cross didn't He?"

"Yes, on the third day," I remarked.

My dad asked, "And then what?"

I said, "He went back to Heaven."

My dad said, "Good. And He's coming back again someday isn't He?"

"Yes," I said. "Dad, I look forward to being with God, where I can see Him."

My dad assured me, "He looks forward to that day too Sarah. Hey, you look sleepy. Why don't we pray and thank God for who He is, the evidence He's provided us, and for our family and friends who don't yet know Him in a personal way."

Additional Books and DVDs by Charlie Campbell for ages 13 and up...

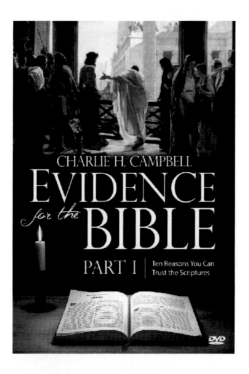

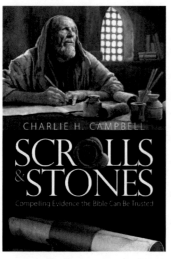

Evidence for the Bible (DVD)

Was the Bible written by deceitful men? Is the Bible out-of-sync with scientific discoveries? Has the Bible undergone corruption as it was translated down through the centuries? Are the persons, places and events mentioned in the Bible mythological? What sets the Bible apart from other religious writings like the Quran, Hindu Vedas, or Book of Mormon? Charlie Campbell has been researching answers to questions like these for more than twenty years. In this updated, expanded, third edition DVD he answers these questions as he builds a compelling ten-pronged case for the trustworthiness of the Bible. In this visual PowerPoint presentation, you'll learn about...

- Scientific Discoveries
- Archaeological Evidence
- Fulfilled Prophecies
- The Dead Sea Scrolls
- Extrabiblical Historical Sources
- The Martyrdom of the Disciples
- Jesus' View of the Scriptures
- The Church Fathers
- Problems in the Quran
- Problems in the Book of Mormon

DVD Length: 83 minutes.

Scrolls and Stones (Book):
Compelling Evidence the Bible Can Be Trusted

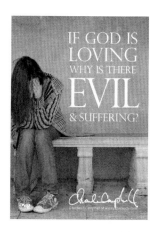

If God is Loving, Why is there Evil and Suffering? (DVD)

Daily we are confronted with headlines about wars, famines, earthquakes, disease, tsunamis, terrorists, refugees, and death. If God existed, surely He would not allow these things to exist or to continue…or would He? And if so, why? Couldn't He prevent some of these things? Couldn't He have made a better world? In this DVD, Charlie Campbell answers these and several other tough theological questions related to evil and suffering. If you've wrestled with these questions yourself, this DVD will be comforting and instructive; but it will also help equip you to reason with atheists and other critics of the Bible who think evil and suffering disprove God's existence. 51 minutes.

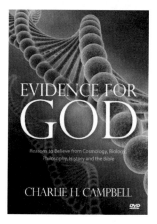

Evidence for God (DVD)

Did the universe just pop into being from nothing, like Richard Dawkins and other prominent atheists say? Did human beings with 206 bones and 640 muscles come into being by unguided natural causes? Searching out answers to questions like these led Charlie Campbell to abandon his atheism in 1990. In this DVD, he shares some of the evidence from cosmology, biology, philosophy, history, and the Bible that changed his mind. 68 minutes.

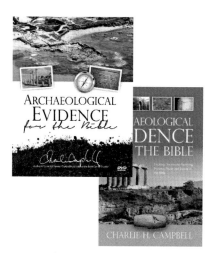

Archaeological Evidence for the Bible (Book or DVD)

Is the Bible a collection of fables and myths? Are the persons, places, and events in the Bible just fabrications by deceitful men? Many critics of Christianity think so, but archaeological discoveries show otherwise. Over the past two centuries, archaeologists have made thousands of discoveries that have helped to verify the exact truthfulness of the Bible's detailed records of various events, customs, persons, cities, nations, and geographical locations. This DVD by Charlie Campbell will introduce you to several of these fascinating Bible-affirming finds, both old and new. DVD is 53 minutes. Full color book is 150 pages.

These and dozens of other resources by Charlie Campbell are available today at AlwaysBeReady.com.

CHARLIE CAMPBELL

Charlie Campbell resides in southern California with his wife and five kids. He is the founder of AlwaysBeReady.com, a popular Christian apologetics website. His DVDs and books on evidence for God, evidence for the Bible, religions, and cults, are used in Bible colleges, Sunday school classrooms, and home fellowships all over the world.

Website: **AlwaysBeReady.com**
Email: **info@alwaysbeready.com**
Instagram: **charlie_h_campbell**
Twitter: **@CharlieABReady**

JULIA VEENSTRA

Julia Veenstra is a wife and the mother of five children. Drawing and painting has always been a part of her life. After receiving formal training in illustration in Canada she opened a studio in her home and has been freelancing ever since. Her "home" has included residency in Canada, her birthplace, and the United States as well as a five year missionary status in Tanzania and Kenya. She has been able to use her talents in ministry, teaching art to students, and personal tent making. Her painting and drawing always continue to develop and she loves the "expression" of paint. Her family sometimes tire of her random outbursts of joy over color!

Website: **JuliaVeenstra.com**
Email: **veenstra@juliaveenstra.com**
Instagram: **jveenstraartist**
Twitter: **@jveenstraartist**

"Some atheists are trying to pull down anything that reminds people of God. But they will never pull down the stars."
–Charlie Campbell

"The chief reason people do not know God is not because He hides from them but because they hide from Him."
–John Stott

"To sustain the belief that there is no God, atheism has to demonstrate infinite knowledge, which is tantamount to saying, 'I have infinite knowledge that there is no being in existence with infinite knowledge.'"
–Ravi Zacharias

"I am persuaded that men think there is no God because they wish there were none. They find it hard to believe in God, and to go on in sin, so they try to get an easy conscience by denying his existence."
–Charles Spurgeon

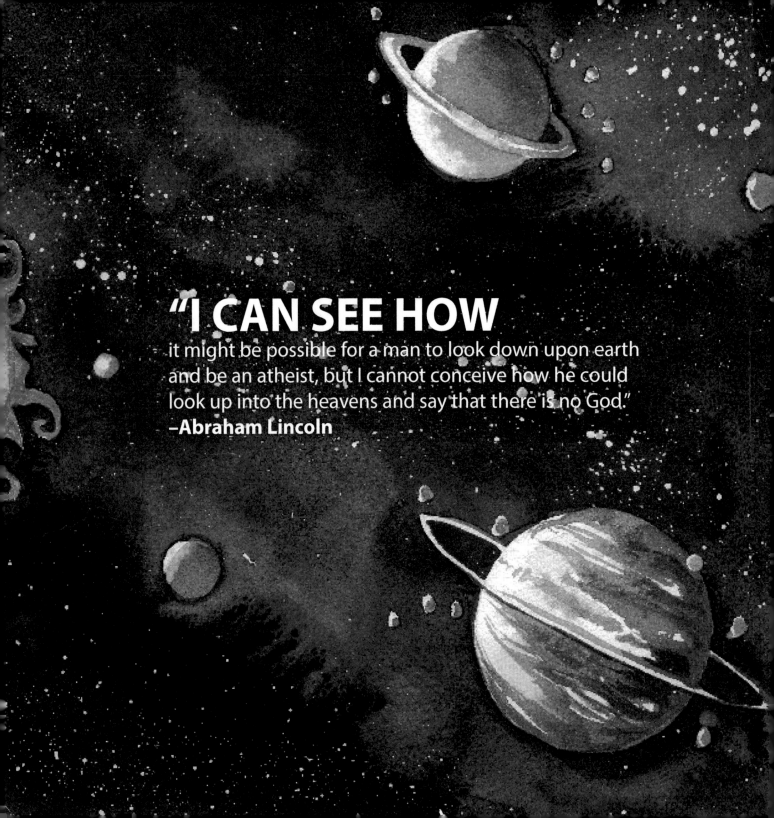

"I CAN SEE HOW
it might be possible for a man to look down upon earth and be an atheist, but I cannot conceive how he could look up into the heavens and say that there is no God."
–Abraham Lincoln

Made in the USA
San Bernardino, CA
18 September 2017